S0-EAJ-223

The Development of Antidepressants

The Chemistry of Depression

ANTIDEPRESSANTS

ANTIDEPRESSANTS

The Development of Antidepressants

The Chemistry of Depression

by Maryalice Walker

Mason Crest Publishers

Philadelphia

Mason Crest Publishers Inc.
370 Reed Road
Broomall, Pennsylvania 19008
(866) MCP-BOOK (toll free)

First printing
1 2 3 4 5 6 7 8 9 10

Library of Congress Cataloging-in-Publication Data

Walker, Maryalice.
  The development of antidepressants : the chemistry of depression / by Maryalice Walker.
      p. cm. — (Antidepressants)
  Includes bibliographical references and index.
  ISBN 1-4222-0102-3   ISBN 1-4222-0094-9 (series)
  1. Depression—Treatment—Juvenile literature. 2. Antidepressants—Physiological effect—Juvenile literature. I. Title. II. Series.
  RM315.W29 2007
  615'.78—dc22
                                2006005484

Interior design by MK Bassett-Harvey.
Interiors produced by Harding House Publishing Service, Inc.
www.hardinghousepages.com.
Cover design by Peter Culatta.
Printed in the Hashemite Kingdom of Jordan.

This book is meant to educate and should not be used as an alternative to appropriate medical care. Its creators have made every effort to ensure that the information presented is accurate—but it is not intended to substitute for the help and services of trained professionals.

Contents

Introduction

by Andrew M. Kleiman, M.D.

From ancient Greece through the twenty-first century, the experience of sadness and depression is one of the many that define humanity. As long as human beings have felt emotions, they have endured depression. Experienced by people from every race, socioeconomic class, age group, and culture, depression is an emotional and physical experience that millions of people suffer each day. Despite being described in literature and music; examined by countless scientists, philosophers, and thinkers; and studied and treated for centuries, depression continues to remain as complex and mysterious as ever.

In today's Western culture, hearing about depression and treatments for depression is common. Adolescents in particular are bombarded with information, warnings, recommendations, and suggestions. It is critical that adolescents and young people have an understanding of depression and its impact on an individual's psychological and physical health, as well as the treatment options available to help those who suffer from depression.

Why? Because depression can lead to poor school performance, isolation from family and friends, alcohol and drug abuse, and even suicide. This doesn't have to be the case, since many useful and promising treatments exist to relieve the suffering of those with depression. Treatments for depression may also pose certain risks, however.

Since the beginning of civilization, people have been trying to alleviate the suffering of those with depression. Modern-day medicine and psychology have taken the understanding and treatment of depression to new heights. Despite their shortcomings, these treatments have helped millions and millions of people lead happier, more fulfilling and prosperous lives that would not be possible in generations past. These treatments, however, have their own risks, and for some people, may not be effective at all. Much work in neuroscience, medicine, and psychology needs to be done in the years to come.

Many adolescents experience depression, and this book series will help young people to recognize depression both in themselves and in those around them. It will give them the basic understanding of the history of depression and the various treatments that have been used to combat depression over the years. The books will also provide a basic scientific understanding of depression, and the many biological, psychological, and alternative treatments available to someone suffering from depression today.

Each person's brain and biology, life experiences, thoughts, and day-to-day situations are unique. Similarly, each individual experiences depression and sadness in a unique way. Each adolescent suffering from depression thus requires a distinct, individual treatment plan that best suits his or her needs. This series promises to be a vital resource for helping young people recognize and understand depression, and make informed and thoughtful decisions regarding treatment.

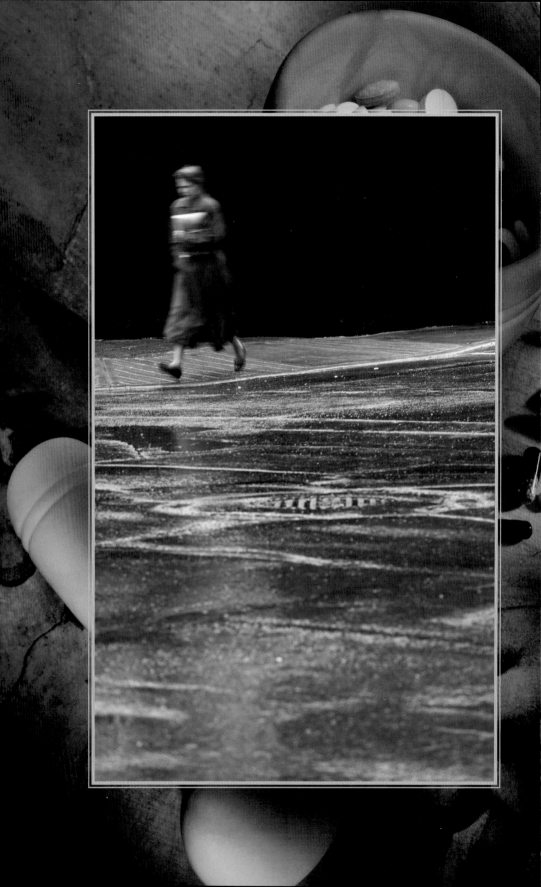

Chapter 1

Blue Days

The patient entered the examination room and slowly lowered herself into the chair across from the doctor; concerned by her sudden change in mood, she had decided to have a checkup. When the doctor asked her how she was feeling, the patient replied that she felt sad and despondent, and often experienced great difficulty just getting out of bed in the morning. Usually the first person in her family to wake up, she had for the past few months been sleeping into the afternoon despite the alarm clock she set. Once described by her friends and family as "bubbly, outgoing, and *optimistic*," the patient now described her outlook as hopeless, as if her life no longer had any meaning. Prior to this drop in mood, she had been an avid mountain climber and skier. However, she told the doctor she no longer had any interest in either hobby, nor did she enjoy spending time with her usual friends. The patient summarized her general feeling with the statement, "I cry all the time and I do not know why."

After talking with her doctor, the patient also met with a psychiatrist, a special type of medical doctor with an expertise in psychological problems. The psychiatrist was able to confirm that the changes in mood and behavior the patient described were common symptoms, or signs, of a clinical disorder called depression.

What Is Depression?

Depression is one of the most common major **mood disorders** and involves changes in a person's emotions, behavior, and thought patterns, changes that are strong enough to disrupt a person's usual functioning for six months or more. Depression impacts the way a person feels about himself, how he thinks, and even how he eats and sleeps. Although depression may seem like a temporary "down-in-the-dumps" mood, the sufferer cannot simply "cheer up" after a while. Some symptoms of depression include:

- feelings of extreme sadness, emptiness, anxiety

- thoughts of hopelessness, helplessness

- thoughts of suicide, suicide attempts

- loss of interest in usual activities, such as hobbies, school, or work

- loss of appetite or overeating

- oversleeping or waking up unusually early, and difficulty sleeping

- loss of concentration, difficulty remembering

- fatigue

- restlessness or irritability

- physical symptoms such as headaches, backaches, and digestive trouble that do not improve with medical treatment

A person who is depressed may overeat as a way of coping with his emotions.

Not everyone who is depressed suffers all of these symptoms, however; according to the *Diagnostic and Statistical Manual for Mental Disorders* or DSM, a person must suffer from at least five of the above symptoms for more than two weeks. Everyone gets sad now and then, but unlike a usual "blue" mood, the symptoms of depression may last for weeks, months, or even, in some cases, years. A person with depression typically experiences depressive episodes, periods during which she is depressed, several times over the course of her life.

Whom Does Depression Affect?

Depression may occur in the young and old, male and female. According to the National Institute of Mental Health, as many as 18.8 million adults in the United States may suffer from depression in a given year. That is 9.5 percent of the total population. The National Institute of Mental Health estimates depression affects between three and four million men—and about twice as many women.

Depression in women may take several forms, such as postpartum depression, a type of depression that occurs after childbirth; depression during pregnancy; and premenstrual dysphoric disorder (PMDD), a depression associated with a high sensitivity to changing hormone levels just before menstruation. Depression during pregnancy is difficult to diagnose because its symptoms may be confused with usual changes that occur during pregnancy, such as changes in appetite and sleeping habits. Of course, women may suffer depression outside of pregnancy, childbirth, and the menstrual cycle.

The hormonal changes during pregnancy
may cause feelings of sadness.

Depression in men occurs less frequently than in women, and men are less likely to report being depressed, just as doctors are less likely to recognize depression in men, according to the National Institute of Mental Health. One reason a doctor may not recognize some symptoms of depression in men is because these symptoms, such as working very late hours, may be seen as socially acceptable. Symptoms of depression in men are often different from those in women. Women with depression often feel helpless or hopeless, but men tend to show depression with increased irritability, anger, and discouragement, all of which can be hidden by alcohol and drug abuse. The National Institute of Mental Health has launched a campaign to increase society's awareness of depression in men and dispel the social myth that men do not suffer depression.

Depression in adolescents may be difficult to detect because the symptoms can hide behind emotional, behavioral, and physical changes typically associated with adolescence. However, excessive sleeping, irritability, moodiness, an uncharacteristic loss of interest in school, and thoughts of suicide are all symptoms of depression that should be taken seriously.

While depression is relatively rare in people aged eighty-five years and over, the disorder is nevertheless one of great concern in the elderly population. Contrary to popular belief, depression in the elderly is not usual. While most of the elderly population still enjoys a fulfilling life, some elderly people suffer depression as a result of a physical illness such

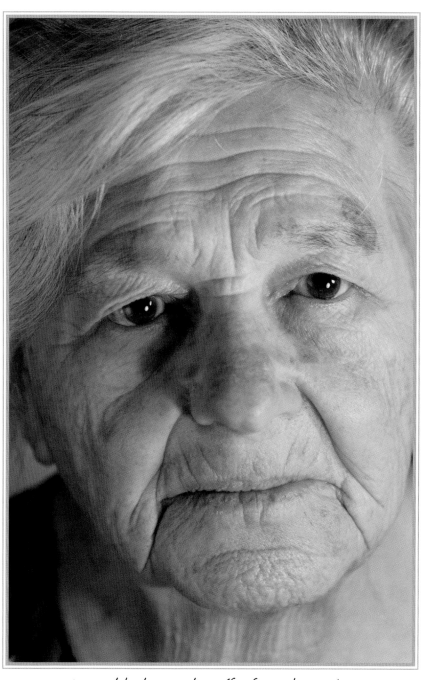

*Some elderly people suffer from depression
as a result of physical illnesses.*

Alcohol abuse can contribute to depression.

as cancer or ***Parkinson's disease***, or as a side effect of certain medications. However, the symptoms of depression in the elderly often go unrecognized because many elderly patients report the physical and not the emotional symptoms of depression. Determining whether the elderly patient has depression or is instead depressed due to an illness or the side effects of a medication is an important skill for doctors.

What Causes Depression?

The cause of depression has eluded scientists for more than fifty years; however, scientists today emphasize that more than one if not several factors may cause depression. The likelihood that a person will suffer from depression is determined by interactions between a person's biology, psychology, and environment. Several factors may influence the probability that an individual will develop depression:

- genetics
- social or environmental conditions
- thought patterns
- insecure attachments
- physical conditions such as illness
- individual vulnerability and stress
- alcohol and substance abuse

A family history of depression may make someone more vulnerable or predisposed to developing the disorder. In other words, some physical changes in the brain associated with depression can sometimes be passed down genetically from one generation to the next. However, not all people with a genetic vulnerability to depression develop the disorder, just as people without a genetic vulnerability to depression may nevertheless experience depression.

Social theories on the cause of depression focus on stressful events in a person's life. A person who experiences violent or traumatic situations may be more susceptible to developing depression. Other stressful situations such as the loss of a job or financial difficulties may increase the likelihood of having depression. However, these theories do not account for people who lead safe and secure lives but nevertheless develop depression, nor do they explain why most people who experience violence or trauma do not suffer from depression.

In some cases, a person's thinking habits may make her more likely to develop depression. This **cognitive** theory of depression focuses on three **pessimistic** ways of thinking:

- internality

- stability

- lack of control

A depressed person whose thinking habits show internality believes the reason for her unhappiness is inside herself. For example, she may think, "No one wants to talk to me because I am ugly and clumsy," rather than, "People in this office are so focused on themselves and their work, no wonder it is so difficult to make conversation with them." A person whose thought patterns exhibit stability believes her

A model of a DNA strand, which may carry
genetic information that can contribute
to a vulnerability to depression

unhappiness is permanent. She might think, "I will never suc-
ceed." A person whose thought patterns express a lack of control of her situation might believe, "I am miserable because I
am clumsy and I cannot change this."

According to the theory of insecure attachments,
a child who experiences emotional abandonment
may be more prone to depression.

Abraham Lincoln's "Melancholy"

Historians have suggested that Abraham Lincoln suffered from depression throughout his life. Joshua Wolf Shenk, in his book Lincoln's Melancholy: How Depression Challenged a President and Fueled His Greatness, *shows a combination of a family history of mental illness and both stressful events and tragic losses in Lincoln's early life may have contributed to his depression.*

Born on a Kentucky farm on February 12, 1809, Abraham Lincoln had a voracious love for learning that both his father and his neighbors considered unusual for a farm boy. Lincoln left home to live in New Salem, Illinois, at a young age, and though he had only gone to school for one year, he continued to educate himself over the course of his entire life.

When Lincoln began studying harder than before, losing weight, and becoming irritable, his friends in New Salem feared he would commit suicide, so they would not let him out of their sight. The twenty-six-year-old Lincoln had mentioned on several occasions that he wanted to kill himself.

Lincoln's breakdown in 1835 followed a series of losses: the death of his mother, an aunt, and an uncle from "milk sickness" when he was nine years old; the devastating death of his sister, with whom he was very close, in 1828; and finally the death of his friend Anna Mayes Rutledge in 1835.

Could Lincoln have inherited a vulnerability to depression? Both Lincoln's parents had been described by acquaintances as generally sad, and his uncle and cousins were mentally ill.

But depression may not always be a completely negative thing. According to author Joshua Wolf Shenk, Lincoln's melancholy outlook may have given him the strength and clarity of thought to lead the nation through the Civil War.

The theory of insecure attachments focuses on problems with close relationships as a cause of depression. The loss of a loved one, a history of abandonment, separation, or divorce may increase the chances of a person having depression. Alternatively, depression itself may place strain on relationships and ultimately cause them to end.

Physical changes in the body may also make a person more vulnerable to developing depression. Cancer, a stroke, hormonal disorders, and Parkinson's disease are all examples of physical conditions that can lead to depression in which the person experiences feelings of *apathy* and cannot care for himself. The depression can cause him to take longer to recover from his original illness.

The vulnerability–stress explanation for the cause of depression incorporates several of the factors discussed, such as genetic influences, thinking habits, and stressful experiences. The general rule of thumb in thinking about the causes of depression is not to oversimplify: current research emphasizes that depression is the result of the interaction of a number of factors specific to each person's biology, personality, and life experiences.

Scientists have only just begun to make breakthrough discoveries about the biological causes of depression over the last two decades. Much of this research has led to the development of medication that in conjunction with psychotherapy, a type of talk therapy that allows a patient to work through his problems, can help those who suffer the disorder lead a happier, healthier life.

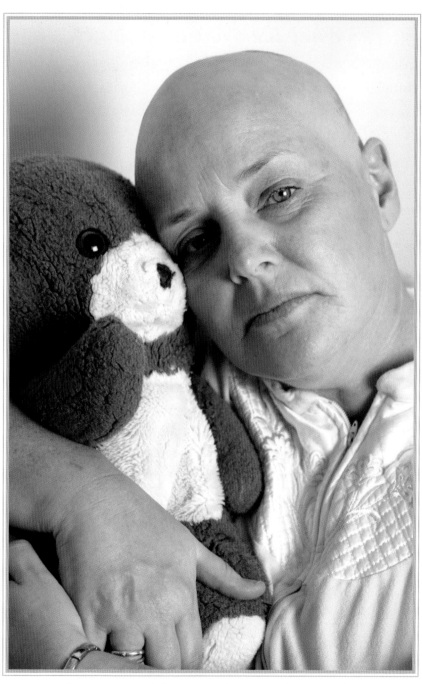

If a person with cancer becomes depressed, it may interfere with her ability to recover.

What Is an Antidepressant?

An antidepressant is a drug used to treat depression. Most antidepressants fall into three main categories based on the chemical structure of the drugs and the way they behave in the human body:

- monoamine oxidase inhibitors (MAOIs)
- selective serotonin reuptake inhibitors (SSRIs) and other serotonin-related medication
- tricyclic antidepressants

Much of the current research on antidepressants was founded on a hypothesis developed in the 1960s called the catecholamine hypothesis. According to this hypothesis, the main biological cause of depression is a chemical imbalance in the brain. When certain brain chemicals that are responsible for maintaining stable moods and emotions become depleted, depression seems to follow. To counteract the depletion of these important chemicals, an effective antidepressant drug should increase the amounts of these chemicals in the brain, helping to restore them to usual levels. The three types of antidepressants listed above work based on this principle, but scientists still do not know exactly how each antidepressant behaves in the brain to alleviate the symptoms of depression. Researchers do know that antidepressants relieve the symptoms of depression, and to find out just how effective each new antidepressant is, they must first test the drugs on those with depression.

Much of the research on the human brain has taken place only during the past fifty years. To find out more about the biological causes of depression and how antidepressants work in the brain, scientists must continue to study its structure and function. Although researchers continue to make ground-breaking discoveries about the way the brain functions, this most important organ of the human body still remains largely a mystery.

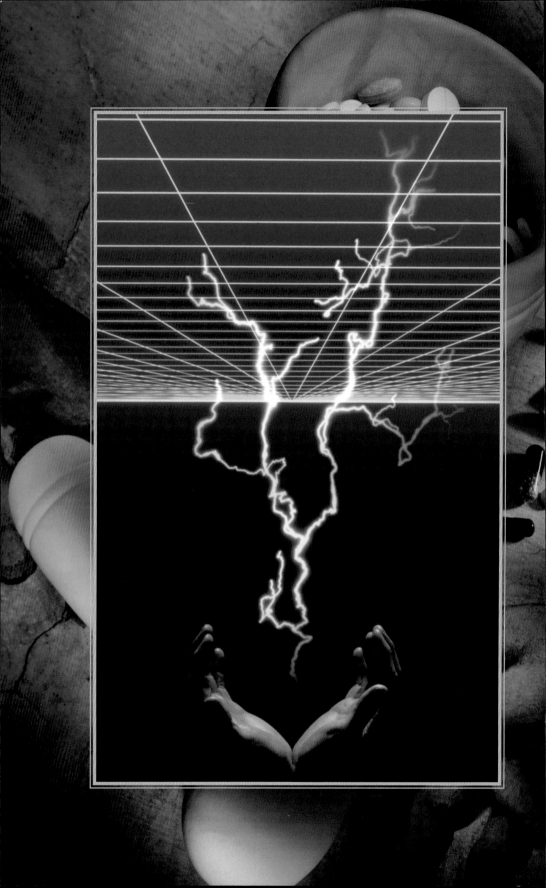

Chapter 2

The Body Electric

Considered to be the seat of our thoughts and emotions, indeed of our consciousness and individuality, the exact ways in which the brain functions still elude scientists. Antidepressants may lessen the symptoms of depression, yet *how* these drugs behave in the brain is largely unknown. To create more effective antidepressants, scientists the world over continue their research to try to understand the structure and function of the human brain.

A Guided Tour of the Brain

Whenever we do the things we love most in life, whether this be listening to music, painting a seaside sunset, or playing basketball with a favorite cousin, we humans have the brain to thank for allowing us to hear and appreciate the music; create beautiful, original art; and get out of that move our cousin uses to try to get the ball from us. The brain is the organ of the human body whose sheer complexity makes us who we are as individuals and sets us apart from other species on earth.

The adult brain weighs just three pounds and makes up only about 2 percent of the body weight of the average human. It rests inside the protection of the skull. Inside the skull, three additional **membranes** protect the brain. The first membrane layer is the *dura mater*, or "hard mother," which contains life-sustaining blood vessels. The second membrane is the *arachnoid*, and even closer to the brain is the *pia mater*,

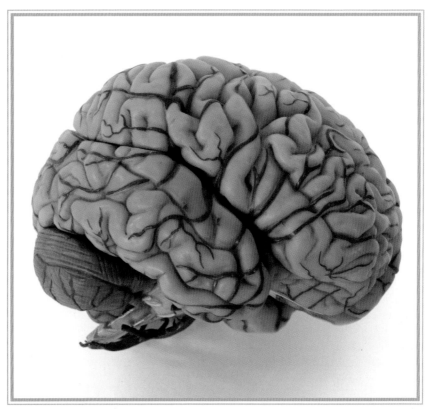

The wrinkled spongy outer surface of the human brain is called the cerebral cortex.

or "tender mother," which is very thin and delicate. A cushioning layer of cerebrospinal fluid between the arachnoid and the pia mater bathes and protects the brain.

Underneath the coverings of membranous tissue is the outer surface of the brain: gray, **convoluted**, and spongy. The "gray matter" on the top and sides of the brain is the cerebral cortex, a layer of tissue less than five millimeters thick that contains the neurons, tiny cells that communicate in a language of electrical and chemical impulses to make thought, movement, and creativity possible. The cerebral cortex contains nearly 75 percent of the cells in the brain.

The brain divides into the right and left **hemispheres**, and within each hemisphere, deep furrows partition the cerebral cortex into four **lobes**:

- frontal lobes
- parietal lobes
- temporal lobes
- occipital lobes

Each lobe is responsible for certain functions. The frontal lobe, located at the front of the brain, make up about half the volume of each hemisphere and contain the regions of the brain that turn a person's thoughts into actions. The frontal lobe contains the motor cortex, which tells all six hundred muscles of the body what to do and when; it also contains Broca's area, a region associated with speech. It's the frontal lobe that allows a hungry person standing at the edge of a stream to figure out how to catch a fish and then carry out her plan by making a fishing rod and performing the necessary movements using the fishing rod to catch her meal. When she succeeds, she can shout, "Yeah!" because of the Broca's area within the frontal lobe. At the very front of the frontal lobes lie regions called the prefrontal lobes, which unite a person's personality with her emotion and make up about 29 percent of the brain's cortex.

At the top of the brain, the parietal lobes receive sensory information such as heat, pressure, and pain from all areas of the body. The temporal lobes at the sides of the brain are involved in emotion, memory, perception, analyzing sounds, and understanding language. At the back of the brain are the occipital lobes associated with sight. It is here where the brain processes visual information.

The brain contains several other specialized regions such as the limbic system, a group of structures at the center of the brain associated with the expression of emotions and memory formation; the thalamus, located deep in the center of the brain and responsible for directing sensory messages from the body to the appropriate parts of the brain; the hypothalamus, located below the thalamus, associated with the elements of basic survival such as hunger, thirst, sex, reproduction, and emotions, as well as the regulation of body temperature; the cerebellum at the back of the brain, responsible for balance and coordination; the pons at the base of the brain, which governs sleep; and the medulla, located near the pons, which is responsible for automatic functions such as breathing and the heartbeat.

Supporting the brain and all its specialized structures is the brain stem at the base of the skull. In the center of the brain stem is a concentrated network of neurons that works its way to the center of the brain. This network is called the reticular activating system (RAS), and it is of great importance because it alerts the specialized regions of the brain to bring incoming information to their attention.

The nervous system, a vast network of pathways to and from the brain, coordinates the receiving of information from the sense organs to the brain and conveys the appropriate responses from the brain to the rest of the body.

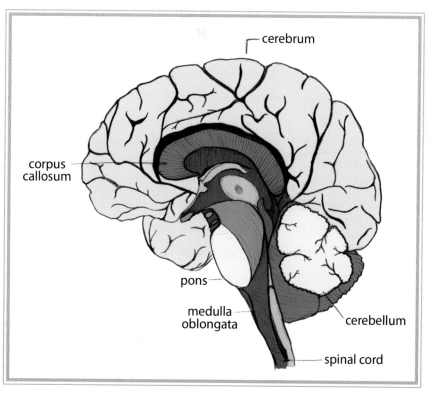

The structure of the human brain

Mapping the Brain

Researchers have developed several techniques to allow a glimpse into the workings of the human brain. One such technique is the PET scan (positron-emission tomography). A PET scan is useful because it gives researchers and doctors a computerized image of activity in the brain.

In the late 1970s, researchers developed the PET scan to gather information about the areas of the brain that are active during certain responses or behaviors. Researchers hoped to discover changes in the brain associated with certain disorders, which would help other scientists develop more effective treatments for these disorders. A PET scan detects the level of activity in certain areas of the brain and displays this information on a visual screen. Glucose is one of many different chemicals that can be visualized and studied with a PET scan.

For the brain to function and thrive, cells in the brain must convert glucose, a sugar, into energy. When cells in a certain area of the brain are very active, they consume glucose at a higher rate to generate the energy they need to keep working. During a PET scan, a scientist injects the patient with a substance that behaves like glucose but also contains a radioactive element. The glucose substance builds up in the more active areas of the brain and emits radiation; it is this radiation that is an indirect indicator of brain activity. A scanning device detects radiation levels in different parts of the brain and generates an image of this brain activity on a screen. For example, a patient going through a period of depression may show low levels of glucose consumption, and thus low activity levels, in a particular part of the brain. However, the cause-and-effect relationship between glucose levels in the brain and depression are not entirely clear, as low glucose levels may bring on depression but depression may also be associated with low brain activity and consequently low glucose consumption.

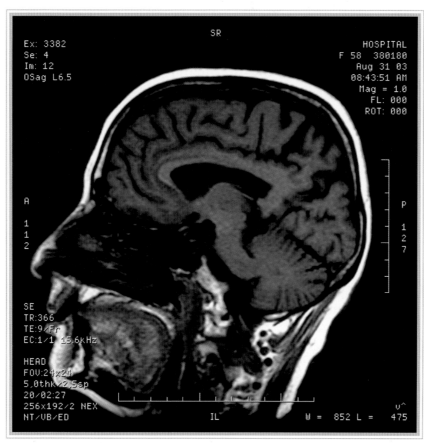

Ex: 3382
Se: 4
Im: 12
OSag L6.5

SR

HOSPITAL
F 58   380180
Aug 31 03
08:43:51 AM
Mag = 1.0
FL: 000
ROT: 000

A

P

1
1
2

1
2
7

SE
TR:366
TE:9/Fr
EC:1/1 15.6kHz

HEAD
FOV:24x24
5.0thk/2.5sp
20/02:27
256x192/2 NEX
NT/VB/ED

IL

W = 852 L =   475

New technology allows us to see inside the human brain.

The Nervous System

The nervous system is an assemblage of billions of cells that collect and process information from inside and outside the body to produce the correct responses to certain **stimuli** and oversee the functions of different cells. The nervous system has two main parts, the central nervous system (CNS) and the **peripheral** nervous system (PNS).

The CNS receives, processes, analyzes, and stores information about incoming sensory experiences such as taste, touch, smell, and color. It sends information to muscles, glands, and the internal organs. The brain and the spinal cord make up the CNS. The spinal cord serves an important purpose as the link between the brain and all of the parts of the body below the neck. It is a delicate assembly of neurons and their associated tissue that runs from the base of the brain down the center of the back and is protected by a column of bones called the spinal column. Neurons, the foundation of the nervous system, communicate with each other in a language of chemical and electrical energy, sending messages to and from the CNS as well as communicating with each other within the CNS.

The PNS is the nervous system outside the brain and spinal cord. Nerves that record sensory information take messages from the skin, muscles, and other internal and external sense organs to neurons in the spinal cord. The neurons in the spinal cord then send these messages to different areas of the brain, which respond appropriately to the messages.

To understand how messages travel between the outside world and the human brain and from the human brain to the rest of the body, it is necessary to take an in-depth look at the body's information-carriers: the neurons.

The Neural Network

The brain is made up of two types of cells: neurons and glial cells. Neurons (which come from the Greek word that means

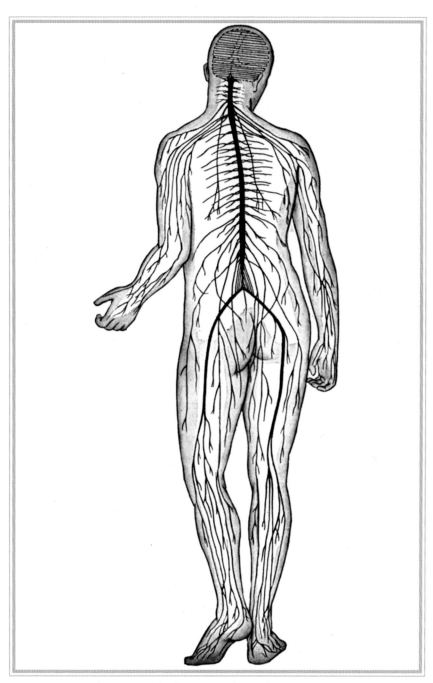

The brain and the spinal cord communicate
with nerves throughout the body.

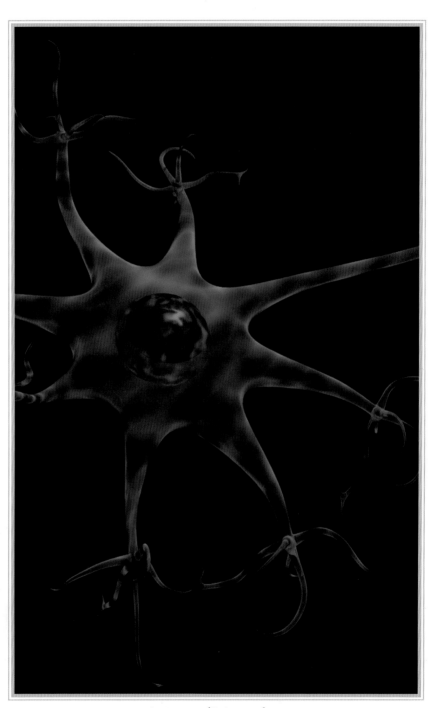

An artist's rendition of a neuron

"to spin"), or nerve cells, are the delicate, microscopic cells responsible for communicating messages within the brain and also to the rest of the human body. Neurons are the cells referred to as "gray matter," because tissue consisting of neurons is in fact gray. The cerebral cortex covering the top and sides of the brain contains about ten billion neurons alone, and these neurons communicate with each other through a complex network of one million billion connections. The entire human brain houses about *one hundred billion* neurons. To picture just how many neurons this is, remember that the Milky Way Galaxy contains about 100 billion stars. Although neurons are responsible for the activity and **dynamism** that occurs within the brain, glial cells (from a Greek word that means "glue") actually outnumber neurons. Glial cells contain the nutrients that keep neurons alive and functioning

Prescription Drug Use in the United States

In 2004, the Department of Health and Human Services reported that almost half of all Americans were taking at least one prescription drug, and that one in six was taking three or more. This represented a 13 percent increase over the number who were taking at least one drug in 1994 and a 40 percent increase in those taking three or more. Five out of every six people over the age of sixty-five took at least one prescription drug every day. Almost half took three or more. Adult use of antidepressants almost tripled between 1994 and 2000. Ten percent of women and 4 percent of men over the age of eighteen take them.

smoothly and also function as the brain's cleanup crew, getting rid of dead nerve cells and other cellular debris.

When a human is born, she possesses all the neurons she will ever have. According to neuroscientist Richard Restak, M.D., between the ages of twenty and fifty, fifty thousand of those neurons will die each day. Fortunately, neurons are quite resourceful cells. As a person grows older and large numbers of neurons die, the remaining neurons will make new connections.

For neurons to communicate with each other, each neuron needs parts that receive messages from other neurons and transmit messages to other neurons. To be able to do this formidable task, a neuron is made up of three parts: the cell body, the dendrites, and the axons. The cell body acts like a receiving and transmitting hub and is shaped like a pyramid or sphere. It has two important roles: keep the neuron alive with the nutrients stored inside it and determine whether the neuron should transmit a message to neighboring neurons. Dendrites extend from the cell body like trees, receiving messages from about 10,000 other neurons and transmitting the messages toward the cell body. Dendrites act like both receivers and transmitters, with a receiving end and a transmitting end. Axons extend anywhere between four-thousandths of an inch up to three feet off the cell body, transmitting messages from the cell body to other neurons as well as muscle and gland cells. A protective fatty covering called a myelin sheath coats the axon and acts as a filter, keeping signals from neighboring cells from interfering with each other. The myelin cov-

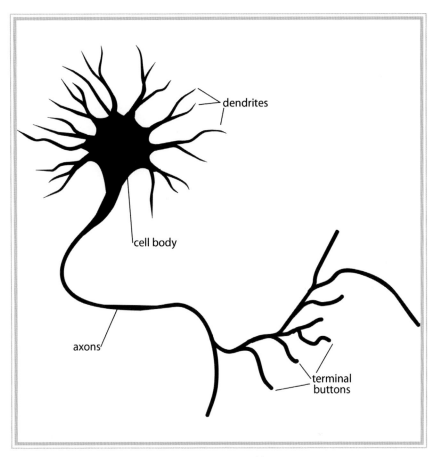

A nerve cell

ering also helps speed up the transmission of messages from one neuron to another.

Neurons communicate with each other through a complex network composed of trillions of connections. Neurons do not actually touch each other but communicate across a gap called a synapse, where the axon of one neuron almost touches the membrane of the cell body or dendrite of another

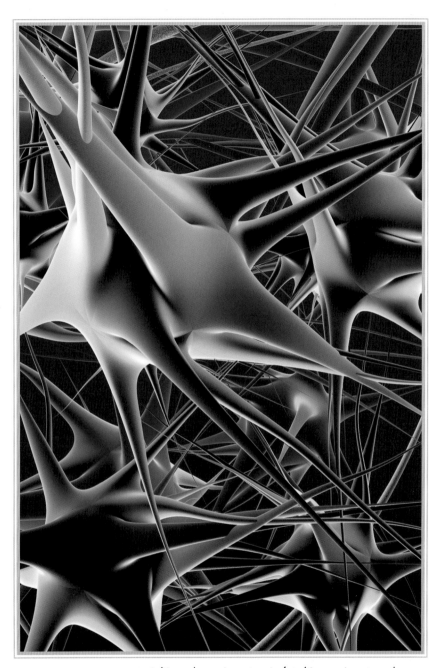

Neurons are not lined up in straight lines; instead,
they interact with each other in a complex web of
relationships, as indicated by this artist's illustration.

neuron. Each axon may branch off hundreds or thousands of times, allowing a single neuron to have many connections to other neurons. As humans grow and develop with age, so do axons and dendrites, so these connections become more and more complex over the years.

When the dendrite of a nerve cell receives information from another nerve cell, what determines whether the axon of a nerve cell that has received this information will send out a message to other nerve cells? The answer to this question lies in the impulses that take place inside the human brain at a rate of 10 million billion times per second. When neurons communicate with each other, messages they send and receive consist of two types of energy: electrical and chemical.

The Body's Electricity

Special proteins in the neurons' cell walls make communication between the nerve cells possible. One type of protein gets

No Straight Lines

Information transfer within the complex network of neurons should be viewed in a nonlinear way. After all, at any one time, each neuron influences 1,000 to 10,000 other neurons. However, concentrating on just one pair of neurons at a time may make understanding the way neurons send and receive messages a little easier.

a neuron ready to send a message. This protein crosses the membrane of the neuron from the outside to the inside and transports electrically charged particles called ions across the neuron's membrane. Two important ions are sodium, which has a negative charge, and potassium, which has a positive charge. Since the function of this protein is to transport sodium and potassium ions into and out of the cell, this protein is called a sodium–potassium pump. When the sodium–potassium pump allows these ions to flow into a neuron, the result is a difference in charge between the inside of the cell and the outside of the cell, with the inside of the neuron becoming more negatively charged than the outside of the neuron. The inside of the cell becomes more negatively charged than the outside of the cell because for every three sodium ions the pump transports out of the cell, it allows only two potassium ions to enter the cell. As a result, the inside of the cell has an electrical charge of about 0.07 **volts** less than the outside of the cell, a difference in energy that creates an electrical potential. The neuron now has the potential to send a message to another neuron in the form of an electrical impulse.

A neuron "fires," or sends a message, when the voltage difference between the inside and the outside of the cell membrane decreases. This decrease in voltage results from a domino effect emanating from other neurons: when the voltage of one neuron changes, this electrical disruption **propagates** along the axon outward to the membranes of other neurons. When the membrane of the receiving neuron reaches a certain electrical charge, a second special type of protein called an ion

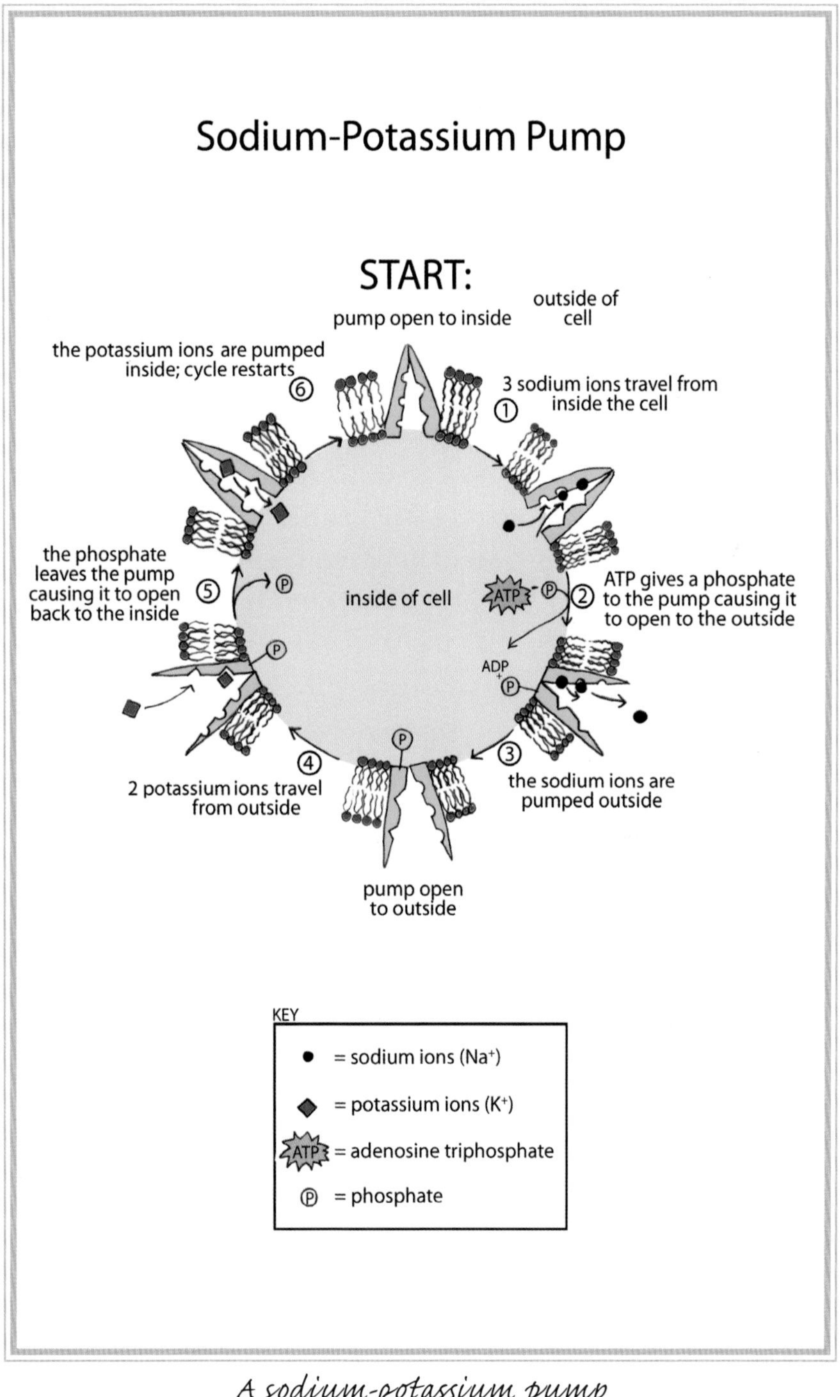

Sodium-Potassium Pump

START:
pump open to inside

outside of cell

the potassium ions are pumped inside; cycle restarts ⑥

3 sodium ions travel from inside the cell ①

the phosphate leaves the pump causing it to open back to the inside ⑤

Ⓟ

inside of cell

ATP Ⓟ ②

ATP gives a phosphate to the pump causing it to open to the outside

ADP + Ⓟ

Ⓟ

Ⓟ

④

Ⓟ

③

2 potassium ions travel from outside

the sodium ions are pumped outside

pump open to outside

KEY

●	= sodium ions (Na⁺)
◆	= potassium ions (K⁺)
ATP	= adenosine triphosphate
Ⓟ	= phosphate

A sodium-potassium pump

The Discovery of Chemical Messengers in the Brain

In 1970, Dr. Julius Axelrod received a Nobel Prize in Physiology or Medicine for his research on the biological causes of depression. He shared the prize with researchers Sir Bernard Katz of the United Kingdom and Ulf von Euler of Sweden.

A scientist at the National Institute of Health for fifty years, Dr. Axelrod is well known for his research on brain chemistry in the early 1960s, as he laid the foundation for the current understanding of depression and anxiety disorders. In his Nobel Prize–winning work, Dr. Axelrod discovered how neurons communicate with each other. He described the way neurons release neurotransmitters, chemicals used to transmit messages between neurons, and how neurons also take these chemicals back in. Neurons can make these chemicals more or less available for communication, either sending out an important message to other neurons or "putting on the brakes," by taking the chemicals back in so as not to overload the brain's circuits. The process by which neurons take these chemicals back in is called reuptake.

Dr. Axelrod's discovery of the reuptake mechanism in neurons led to the development of antidepressants used today. These antidepressants help regulate the amount of neurotransmitters being taken back into the neurons of the brain. Dr. Axelrod called these sorts of drugs reuptake inhibitors because they prevent neurons from taking these important chemicals back in, thus making more of them accessible for communication in a brain in which not enough of these chemicals are available.

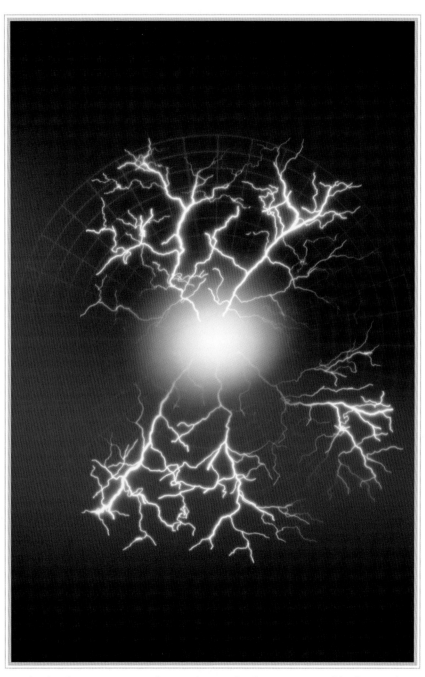

*Like lightning traveling through the nerve cells' branches,
the body has its own complicated electrical system.*

channel protein changes shape to allow sodium or potassium ions to cross the cell membrane of the neuron. Sodium channel proteins open to allow sodium ions into the cell, giving the inside of the neuron's cell membrane along the axon a positive charge. Then sodium ion channels close and potassium ion channels open to allow potassium ions to flow out of the cell, resulting in a decrease in the positive charge within the axon until the inside of the cell has a negative charge that is once again 0.07 volts less than that of the outside of the cell membrane. This alternating process in which the inside of the cell gains and loses electrical charge is the action potential. The action potential repeats along the length of a neuron's axon toward the neuron that will receive the message.

Nerve cells magnified many thousands of times

For an electrical impulse to send information across a synapse, however, the message must be sent in the form of chemical energy. The composition and transmission of these chemical messages has been the focus of research into the causes and treatments of depression for more than four decades.

Chapter 3

Chemical Messengers

The intrepid foreign vacationer awoke on a bright summer day in Spain and decided to go to the beach. After all, the sun was warm, the sky was clear, and he needed to stretch his legs. Today would be a good day to take a long walk or play some volleyball, he thought. So he packed his backpack and walked down to the ocean, where crowds of people like himself relaxed in the sun, took walks on the soft sand, played in the waves, and tossed Frisbees. He found a game of volleyball to join, and he enjoyed the sport and his new volleyball friends until sunset. At the end of the day, his team had won most of the games. Smiling, laughing, and talking, the volleyball teams congratulated each other on a tournament well played.

The happily vacationing tourist was probably not aware of the complex functioning of his brain that allowed him to play volleyball while enjoying the sights, smells, and sounds of the beach on a summer day. His billions of nerve cells and their information networks made possible his emotions of happiness and satisfaction by communicating with each other through a combination of electrical and chemical signals. When nerve cells of the brain "talk" to each other, they transform the information contained in electrical impulses to chemical energy. Nerve cells send out molecules of special chemicals called neurotransmitters that carry messages to other neurons in particular parts of the brain and affect everything from a person's heartbeat and muscle contractions to his emotions and behavior.

Some of these chemicals are very important in studying and treating depression. Only in the last half of the twentieth century did scientists discover and begin to learn more about the brain chemicals that play important roles in psychiatric disorders.

What Is a Neurotransmitter?

In general, a neurotransmitter is a chemical that conveys signals between neurons of the brain. Some neurotransmitters are large and some are very small. Neurotransmitters are made up of between one and thirty-six amino acids and are categorized by their size, or the number of amino acids they contain. Amino acids are the building blocks of proteins and contain atoms of hydrogen, oxygen, nitrogen, carbon, and sulfur. One group of neurotransmitters, the large neuropeptides, consists of more than three amino acids bonded together in a chain. The smaller neurotransmitters that tend to consist of just one amino acid are logically named small-molecule neurotransmitters.

By the 1960s, scientists had discovered several neurotransmitters:

- acetylcholine

- dopamine

- epinephrine

Just as each individual player's baskets contribute to the overall team score, all the neurotransmitters released by the neurons add up to a larger message.

- norepinephrine
- serotonin
- glutamate
- gamma-aminobutyric acid (GABA)
- glycine

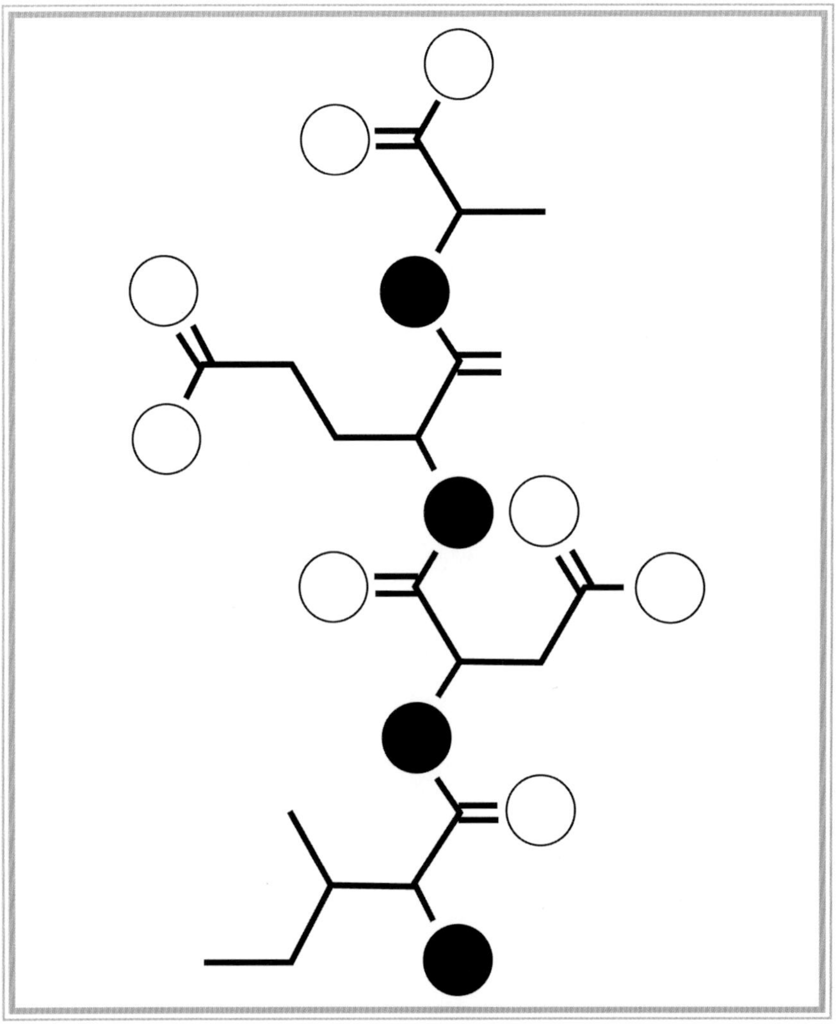

Amino acids exist in chain-like structures.

Legendary Discoveries:

Things That Go Thump-Thump in the Night

At the turn of the twentieth century, one of the major scientific problems facing researchers who studied the brain was how neurons communicated with each other. The popularly accepted hypothesis at the time was that neurons communicated through unbroken electrical impulses. However, some scientists in the early twentieth century challenged this hypothesis, suggesting nerve cells communicated with each other by releasing chemicals. In 1926, a German scientist named Otto Loewi made a breakthrough discovery that earned more support for the chemical transmission hypothesis and earned Dr. Loewi a Nobel Prize in 1936.

According to popular legend, Dr. Loewi thought of the idea for his experiment in the middle of the night and rushed to the lab to complete it in the wee hours of the morning. He placed two fresh frog hearts in a special electrically neutral solution called Ringer's solution and recorded the beat rate of both hearts. When he stimulated the vagus nerve of one of the hearts with an electric current, the heartbeat slowed down. He then collected solution from around this heart and injected it into the solution surrounding the second heart, which did not receive any electrical stimulation. When the second heart began beating slower, too, Dr. Loewi was able to suggest that the vagus nerve regulates heartbeat by releasing some sort of chemical. He had discovered a neurotransmitter that would become known as acetylcholine. Today acetylcholine is the most thoroughly researched neurotransmitter.

Now, just over forty years later, scientists know of more than one hundred neurotransmitters.

The three major neurotransmitters involved in the current treatment of depression are serotonin, norepinephrine, and, to a lesser extent, dopamine. These chemicals are small-molecule neurotransmitters. They are also known as mono-amines, because they consist of a single amino acid.

During signal transmission, neurotransmitters go through a basic process or cycle between the neuron that sends the message and the neuron that receives it. This process involves the neuron producing its own neurotransmitters, sending them to another neuron, and then taking them back up to

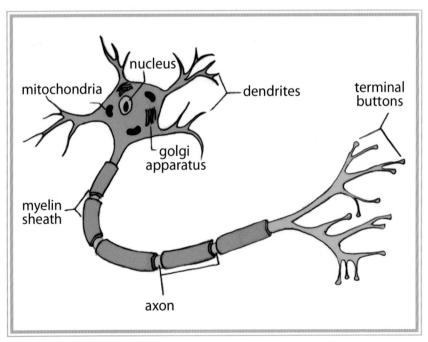

Neurotransmitters are released by the
terminal buttons on a nerve cell.

stop the signal transmission. By sending out neurotransmitters and taking them back, neurons regulate when a message travels to a receiving neuron and for how long that signal lasts.

Neurons Make Their Own Neurotransmitters

Neurons manufacture their own neurotransmitters. The materials and processes a neuron uses to make them depend on the type of neurotransmitter the neuron produces. Neurons that release the small neurotransmitters involved in depression manufacture them with the aid of specialized proteins that bring chemical building blocks into the neuron and others that help spur on the chemical reactions that ultimately produce serotonin, norepinephrine, and dopamine.

Proteins that cross the neuron's cell membrane allow the chemical building blocks that create neurotransmitters to enter the nerve cell. Enzymes, which are special proteins that help build and break down molecules, use these chemical building blocks to manufacture neurotransmitters. For example, the neurotransmitter serotonin, which is involved in regulating mood, sleep, and appetite, comes from tryptophan, an amino acid that is important in the diet and found in foods like turkey, nuts, and bananas. Tryptophan is an essential dietary requirement because the human body cannot make this amino acid on its own. Membrane proteins transport tryptophan into the neuron where it undergoes a chemical reaction to form 5-hydroxytryptamine, or serotonin, also known as

Mood, Munchies, and Mayhem

The neurotransmitters serotonin and norepinephrine regulate several biological processes. Serotonin regulates mood, appetite, impulsive behavior, aggression, and sleep. The role of serotonin is to inhibit, or down-regulate, these body functions and behaviors. Without enough serotonin, a typically content person might become moody and irritable. He may take dangerous risks or become aggressive. For example, if he were to go out to dinner at a restaurant, he might sulk and snap at the waiter during the appetizers, eat two large main courses, and get into a fistfight over the price of baked beans with the person at the table next to him; and all this before dessert! Too much serotonin, however, could cause him to become much happier and more energetic than usual. He might sleep very little. Over the same restaurant meal, he might talk constantly and excitedly, picking at his food and eating very little.

Norepinephrine, takes an opposite role to that of serotonin when it regulates sleep, wakefulness, attention, focus, and eating habits. For example, a woman sitting in the same restaurant might eat very little for dinner, quarrel with the man at the other table over the color of his socks rather than over his foul mood, and find sleeping impossible once she arrives at her home because she has too little norepinephrine.

The general hypothesis about how antidepressant drugs work is based on this notion of a chemical balance in the brain. Depression involves a shortage of one or more neurotransmitters like serotonin and norepinephrine. Antidepressants increase levels of these neurotransmitters to lift mood and bring other habits such as eating and sleeping back to usual patterns.

A turkey dinner contains tryptophan, an amino acid that helps regulate sleep and mood.

5-HT. Norepinephrine, on the other hand, begins as dopamine, a neurotransmitter involved in addiction and disorders such as ***schizophrenia***. With the help of a specialized enzyme, dopamine undergoes chemical reactions to produce norepinephrine. Once a neuron manufactures its signaling chemicals, these chemicals can be released to transmit a message to other neurons.

*Scientists found that protein played
a role in mouse depression.*

Depressed Mice?

Could a protein in the brains of depressed mice be the key to developing more successful antidepressants? Dr. Paul Greengard, a Nobel Prize–winning scientist, and his colleagues at the National Institute of Mental Health discovered a protein that helps regulate serotonin in the mouse brain.

In the study released in 2005, the scientists found that p11 helps bring serotonin receptors to the surface of nerve cells. The team compared p11 levels in humans and mice without depression to humans with depression and mice that showed symptoms similar to depression in humans, such as slow movement and low activity levels. When humans and mice with depression showed significantly lower levels of the protein than those of humans and mice without depression, the scientists hypothesized that p11 might play a role in depression.

If the protein played a role in depression, giving antidepressants to the mice with lower p11 levels, the scientists thought, would increase their p11 levels. Conversely, lowering p11 levels in healthy mice would bring on depression. When the results of these tests confirmed their hypothesis, Dr. Greengard and his team carried out one last experiment to find out just how much the p11 protein influences serotonin receptors. The scientists eliminated the gene that codes for p11 in a group of mice; these mice would be left without the protein. Results of this test showed that the mice had fewer serotonin receptors of a particular kind called 5-HT1B. As a consequence, these mice had lower levels of serotonin and behaved lethargically. Without protein p11, the mice were depressed.

Just how antidepressants increase p11 levels remains unknown; however, the results of this study are important because the p11 protein may provide another way for scientists to target and treat depression.

Releasing Neurotransmitters

When a neuron releases neurotransmitters, it acts a bit like a letter carrier with a bag full of mail who must deliver his messages to the right addresses. Neurotransmitters, which carry the important messages, are packaged in vesicles. Vesicles are small membranous sacs just forty to 120 nanometers in diameter. (One nanometer is one millionth of one millimeter.) These "mail bags" store and release neurotransmitters.

The Short Life of a Neurotransmitter

1. Enzymes aid chemical reactions to produce neurotransmitters inside the neuron's cell body or the end of the axon.

2. Neurotransmitters become packaged inside membranous vesicles.

3. Vesicles fuse with the cell membrane and release neurotransmitters into the space between nerve cells.

4. Neurotransmitters cross the synapse and bind to receptors on another neuron.

5. Glial cells "clean up" the neurotransmitters that have done their job, or the neuron takes them back up to be used again.

Neurotransmitters are packaged in tiny bags.

A single vesicle may hold as many as fifteen thousand neurotransmitter molecules! To release their chemical messages, vesicles fuse with the cell membrane of the neuron and secrete their neurotransmitters into the space between nerve cells. The neurotransmitters then travel across the synapse to bind to specific receptor sites on the surface of the receiving nerve cell. Receptors, which are proteins embedded in the membrane of the receiving neuron, only recognize certain neurotransmitters, ensuring that the correct message reaches the correct destination. In this way, receptors are a bit like mailboxes with specific addresses.

Shape Shifters

When neurotransmitters reach the neuron receiving the message, they bind to specific proteins in the membrane of the neuron called receptors. Receptors are complex proteins that take on a several shapes. Each neurotransmitter may have many receptors it "talks" to. Receptors have different specialized roles: some help maintain the right amount of a neurotransmitter in the correct place at the correct time. Receptors have a structure specific to the type of neurotransmitter with which they communicate. When a neurotransmitter binds to a receptor on a message-receiving neuron, the receptor changes shape to let ions into the nerve cell. The binding process changes the electrical charge of the neuron's membrane. The change may be either positive or negative depending on the receptors to which the neurotransmitters bind. For example, a voltage increase in the membrane of the neuron may increase the probability that the neuron will fire off the message in the form of an electrical impulse. Alternatively, the voltage in the membrane of the receiving neuron may decrease when the neurotransmitter binds to the receptor site, decreasing the probability that the neuron will pass on the message.

The message that reaches its final destination depends on several factors, such as the rate at which neurons fire, how many are firing, what types of neurons are firing, and where the neurons are located. Each individual neuron will have many neurotransmitters arriving at its receptors, and each of these neurons will either increase or decrease the

Receptors and neurotransmitters are like locks and keys, designed to exactly "fit" each other.

difference in electrical charge between the inside and the outside of the nerve cell. A neuron essentially averages the positive and negative effects on the electrical charge of its membrane among all of the neurotransmitters arriving at its receptors; it does this about once every millisecond! The neuron uses the average voltage difference between the inside of the neuron and the outside of its cell membrane to decide when to fire. When the difference in electrical charge between the inside and the outside of the cell drops to a certain voltage, the neuron fires off an electrical signal along its axon to stimulate another cycle of neurotransmitter release.

Signal Regulation

Signals in the brain do not always remain "on." If they did, the human body would be on overdrive, without signals to tell it when to sleep or stop eating. When a neuron receiving a message registers that it has gotten enough signals from neurotransmitters, the neurotransmitters become free in the synapses. Through the process called reuptake, free neurotransmitters may return to their original neurons and storage vesicles. In other cases, glial cells may break down excess neurotransmitters left over after a signal is finished. One enzyme in particular breaks down neurotransmitters after they have finished delivering a signal. This enzyme is called monoamine oxidase (MAO), and its function forms the basis for a major class of antidepressants called monoamine oxidase inhibitors (MAOIs).

The specific ways antidepressants affect the brain and treat depression are still largely unknown, but scientists do know that depression generally involves unusually low levels of neurotransmitters such as serotonin and norepinephrine. Antidepressants, therefore, act to increase the levels of these neurotransmitters in the brain, correcting the chemical imbalance.

Chapter 4

Antidepressants at Work

esearch investigators in government laboratories such as the National Institutes of Health (NIH) and in laboratories of pharmaceutical companies such as Novartis, Eli Lilly, and AstraZeneca of Canada work in teams to find compounds that may be useful chemical building blocks for creating new antidepressants (as well as other medications). Antidepressants belong to a class of medications called psychotropic drugs (drugs that act on the brain to affect mood and behavior).

Psychotropic drugs treat depression by altering one or more steps in the process of chemical signaling between neurons, by targeting the manufacture, release, and reuptake of neurotransmitters. By influencing chemicals in the brain, these drugs may change a person's mood, perception, or behavior.

Tricyclic Antidepressants

Tricyclic antidepressants are named for the part of their structure they share in common, a set of three connected rings of carbon. Some tricyclic antidepressants may actually, however, contain between one and four rings of bonded carbon.

Trycyclics get their name from having three connected rings of carbon.

The discovery of tricyclic antidepressants came as a surprise during a search for more effective drugs to treat schizophrenia. Chlorpromazine (Thorazine®) helped calm patients with schizophrenia and lessened the frequency of their **hallucinations**, but scientists wanted to find a more effective form of this drug. Scientists fine-tuned the structure of the drug with the hope that one of the new forms of the medication would have fewer side effects. Scientists investigated the usefulness and effects of one of the drugs, imipramine, in 1957 and 1958. During these early tests, the drug improved the mood and increased the activity level of many of the patients who were depressed, but proved ineffective in treating schizophrenia. After more in-depth studies of the drug, physicians began prescribing the medication as an antidepressant.

Tricyclic antidepressants work by preventing neurons from taking up two neurotransmitters, serotonin and norepinephrine, after they transmit a signal. By impairing the reuptake of serotonin and norepinephrine, the drug increases the availability of these chemicals to act on the brain.

Some examples of tricyclic antidepressants are:

- imipramine (Tofranil®)
- amitriptyline (Elanil®, Endep®)
- clomipramine (Anafranil®)
- doxepin (Adapin®, Sinequan®)
- protriptyline (Vivactil®)

From the 1960s to the 1980s, tricyclic antidepressants were popular. However, the potential for lethal overdose, as well as side effects such as dry mouth, constipation, drowsiness, weight gain, and high blood pressure, rendered them less of a "drug of choice" once pharmaceutical companies developed antidepressants with fewer side effects and a lower risk of death from an accidental overdose.

Monoamine Oxidase Inhibitors (MAOIs)

Quite a bit of luck led to the discovery of MAOIs. While treating patients with tuberculosis, a potentially lethal lung infec-

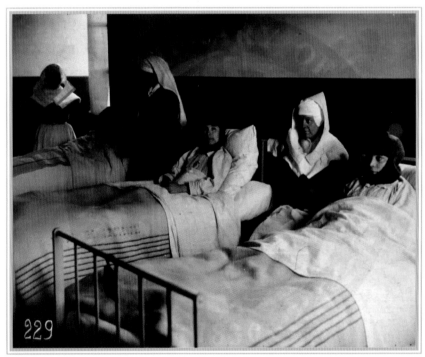

During the nineteenth century and the first half of the twentieth century, patients with tuberculosis were treated in sanitariums. Doctors treating them discovered that an experimental drug, an MAOI, improved their mood and energy level.

tion, interns stumbled on the antidepressant effects of one of the drugs used to treat the infection. Patients who took the drug reported that their mood improved and their energy levels increased after taking the medication. In 1957, scientists studied the drug's effects on depressed patients to find that it indeed had an antidepressant effect. This promising finding led to further studies and the eventual release of the first MAOI.

Like tricyclic antidepressants, MAOIs increase the amount of serotonin and norepinephrine available to act on the brain. However, the way the drugs increase the availability of these chemicals differs from that of the tricyclic medications. Not only did the first MAOI medication prevent tuberculosis-causing bacteria from thriving and spreading, but the drug also stopped the MAO enzyme from breaking down norepinephrine and serotonin after neurons released them, thus leaving

Brand Name vs. Generic Name

Talking about psychiatric drugs can be confusing, because every drug has at least two names: its "generic name" and the "brand name" that the pharmaceutical company uses to market the drug. Generic names come from the drugs' chemical structure, while drug companies use brand names to inspire public recognition and loyalty for their products.

When wine and cheese ferment, they create a protein called tyramine, which can increase heart rate and blood pressure. When a person is taking an MAOI and eats these foods, tyramine can build up in the body to dangerous levels.

more of these neurotransmitters free to continue influencing other neurons.

Although MAOIs may help lessen the symptoms of depression, the benefits of these drugs are not without accompanying drawbacks. Depressed patients taking MAOIs may experience such side effects as dry mouth, constipation, and drowsiness.

The MAOI Cheese Effect

One drawback of MAOI drugs is what is called the "cheese effect." When foods such as cheese, beer, and wine ferment, the chemical process leaves behind a protein called tyramine, which can increase heart rate and blood pressure. When a person who doesn't take an MAOI drug eats cheese, for example, the enzyme MAO in the blood breaks down the tyramine so the protein does not reach harmful levels in the body. In contrast, when a person taking an MAOI drug makes a habit of eating cheese, the action of the drug inhibits the usual function of the MAO enzyme. The MAO enzyme can no longer break down tyramine. As a consequence, tyramine builds up in the person's body and can result in an increase in heart rate and blood pressure great enough to lead to a heart attack or cause blood vessels in the brain to bleed.

The MAO enzyme has two forms, MAOA and MAOB—and the good news is that more recently developed MAOIs can target just one form of the MAO enzyme. The newer MAOIs inactivate MAOA only, leaving MAOB, the enzyme mainly responsible for breaking down tyramine, to do its job. These more selective MAOIs allow patients to eat foods containing tyramine without experiencing its toxic effects.

As with tricyclic antidepressants, MAOIs need some time to take effect. Two to six weeks may pass before patients respond to the drugs with improved mood and greater energy levels. More important, an accidental overdose is likely to be lethal. As a consequence of these risks, scientists began looking for more effective, less toxic antidepressants. The series of antidepressants that resulted from this research are known as selective serotonin reuptake inhibitors or SSRIs.

Selective Serotonin Reuptake Inhibitors (SSRIs)

The development of SSRIs was less of an accidental discovery and more of a methodical research undertaking to find new antidepressant drugs with fewer, and less potent, side effects than the tricyclic drugs and MAOIs. The result of this research was fluoxetine, an SSRI commonly known as Prozac®. This antidepressant emerged from research conducted at Eli Lilly and Company, a major U.S. pharmaceutical company.

Unlike tricyclic drugs, this type of antidepressant is selective; in other words, it acts on serotonin alone. The selectivity of these drugs helps reduce the number of side effects. In addition to having fewer side effects, the SSRIs are safer than tricyclic antidepressants and MAOIs because they are not as lethal if a patient overdoses. Not long after Eli Lilly and Company released the drug in 1987, Prozac become the most widely prescribed antidepressant in North America.

Developing New Antidepressants

Before an antidepressant may be made available to the public, the Food and Drug Administration (FDA) must approve the

SSRIs and Seasonal Affective Disorder (SAD)

In 1993, Dr. Norman Rosenthal at the National Institute of Mental Health in the United States became the first scientist to spread the word about a form of depression called seasonal affective disorder (SAD). Someone with SAD experiences a mood cycle that changes with the seasons in the northern hemisphere. She may be depressed in fall and winter, with symptoms that are not quite the same as major depression. Getting out of bed in the morning will be difficult for her, and she will feel sleepy, sluggish, and slow–moving during the day. She may withdraw from her friends, lose interest in her usual activities, and crave sweet foods that will make her gain weight. In the spring and summer, her depression will lift.

The factors that cause SAD are for the most part unknown, but some studies suggest that light affects the production of serotonin. With fewer hours of daylight and lower levels of serotonin available in the brain, a person with SAD experiences drops in mood. When she receives treatment with an SSRI, a drug that increases serotonin levels, her mood improves and cravings for sugary foods decrease.

Low levels of a chemical called melatonin may also be involved in causing SAD. Melatonin is a hormone that regulates sleep cycles. Melatonin production increases in dark environments, causing sleepiness. Treating a SAD patient with high-powered, full-spectrum light can help her body produce less melatonin to increase her energy levels during the dark days of winter. Hypotheses about the causes of SAD for the most part stem from observations of the methods that effectively treat the disorder.

According to the Mood Disorders Society of Canada, SAD affects between 2 and 4 percent of Canadians. In the United States, about 1 to 2 percent of the population has SAD. Not surprisingly, the number of people with SAD is greatest at northern latitudes where winter days are particularly short. Between 70 and 80 percent of all SAD sufferers are women.

drug. Scientists carry out clinical trials to determine the effectiveness of a newly developed antidepressant. Many organizations and major pharmaceutical companies are involved in testing antidepressant drugs. In a clinical trial, scientists carry out a **controlled**, double-blind, and **randomized** experiment to determine how effectively the antidepressant drug treats the symptoms of depression. Scientists will give either

Drug Approval

Before a drug can be marketed in the United States, the Food and Drug Administration (FDA) must officially approve it. Today's FDA is the primary consumer protection agency in the United States. Operating under the authority given it by the government, and guided by laws established throughout the twentieth century, the FDA has established a rigorous drug approval process that verifies the safety, effectiveness, and accuracy of labeling for any drug marketed in the United States.

While the United States has the FDA for the approval and regulation of drugs and medical devices, Canada has a similar organization called the Therapeutic Product Directorate (TPD). The TPD is a division of Health Canada, the Canadian government department of health. The TPD regulates drugs, medical devises, disinfectants, and sanitizers with disinfectant claims. Some of the things that the TPD monitors are quality, effectiveness, and safety. Just as the FDA must approve new drugs in the United States, the TPD must approve new drugs in Canada before those drugs can enter the market.

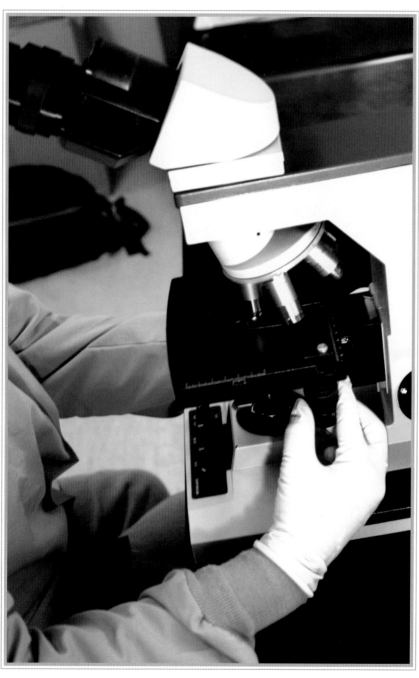

*The production of a new drug involves
years of scientific research.*

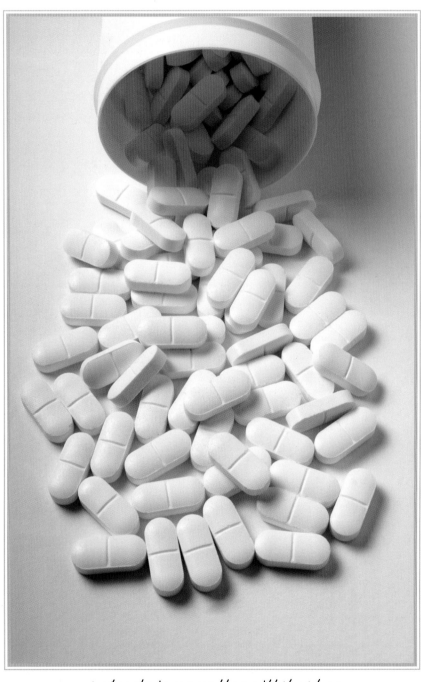

*A placebo is generally a pill that has
no actual medicinal value.*

the antidepressant drug or a placebo (a pill that has no medical effect on the person who takes it) to a random sample of usually more than a hundred people. The scientists monitor their subjects' mental and physical well-being for about six weeks, looking for a difference in the way the subjects react to taking the antidepressant or the placebo. To avoid biasing their results, the experiment is double-blind, meaning neither the scientists who administered the drugs nor the people taking the drugs know which drug has been given to which person. Only the pharmacist involved in the experiment knows this information. At the end of the experiment, the pharmacist reveals which person took which drug so the scientists can analyze the results of the trials. The scientists will need to see if the symptoms of the people who took the antidepressant improved more than those of the people who took the placebo.

Scientists who carry out a clinical trial may find that some of their subjects taking the placebo actually did show a slight improvement in their symptoms. This result is due to a phenomenon called the placebo effect, when the success of a drug or treatment seems to be successful not because of the action of the drug or treatment itself but rather due to the patient's expectations or hopes about how the drug or treatment should make her feel.

Researchers will first undertake a short-term study with a relatively small number of participants. They then review the results of the short-term test to help them design a long-term study with a larger number of subjects.

In the next stage of drug testing, the FDA releases the drug to clinical investigators across the country, who will test the drug's usefulness and safety on a larger number of patients. Clinical investigators will also be looking for ways in which response to the drug varies from person to person in the trials. This study allows researchers to find the final dosage range that is the most therapeutic, or most effective, at treating the symptoms of depression. If the studies show the drug is safe and effective, the FDA gives it conditional approval, meaning the drug may be released for use depending on results from the final stage of clinical trials.

The final drug trials occur under the watchful eyes of physicians who give the drug to their patients and record the effects, including side effects, of the new medication. The FDA monitors the results of the trials and decides, based on these results, whether to allow the pharmaceutical company to market the drug.

By the end of this rigorous series of tests, at least six years may have passed since laboratory scientists first developed the new drug. The strict drug regulations the FDA enforces are important because they protect consumers from receiving potentially harmful substances.

Research on depression and antidepressant drugs is still very young, with most of the major discoveries about the biological causes of depression having occurred over the past fifty years. The discovery of neurotransmitters and the way neurons signal one another, advances in brain research such as PET scans

Final drug trials are carried out by physicians and patients.

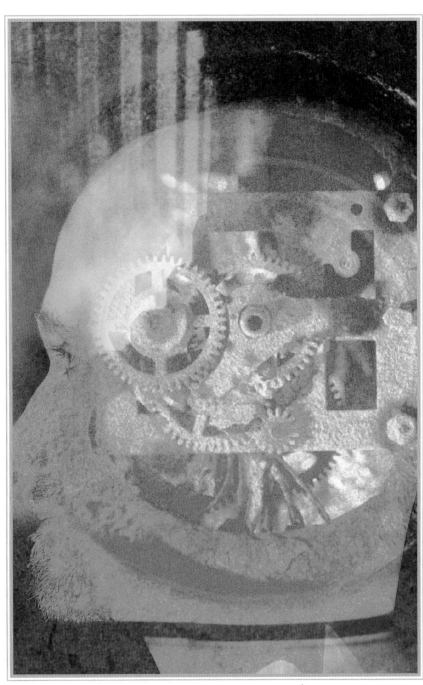

Advances in science give researchers new
windows into the brain's workings.

that give scientists a window into the workings of the brain, and the identification of new structures in the brain that may play a role in depression have all contributed to the development of drugs that are more effective at treating the disorder. Scientists in several diverse fields from chemistry to psychology continue to uncover the complex causes of depression, with the knowledge that a better understanding of how the brain works will lead to more successful medications.

Chapter 5

Careers in Neuroscience and Psychiatry

*E*very day original research in laboratories around the world improves the general understanding of how the human brain functions and the ways in which psychotropic drugs affect it. The development of new antidepressants depends on the concerted, devoted efforts of scientists from many different fields including neuroscience, chemistry, biology, pharmacology, and psychiatry. Within these fields lie a variety of careers that allow scientists to contribute to the research and treatment of depression.

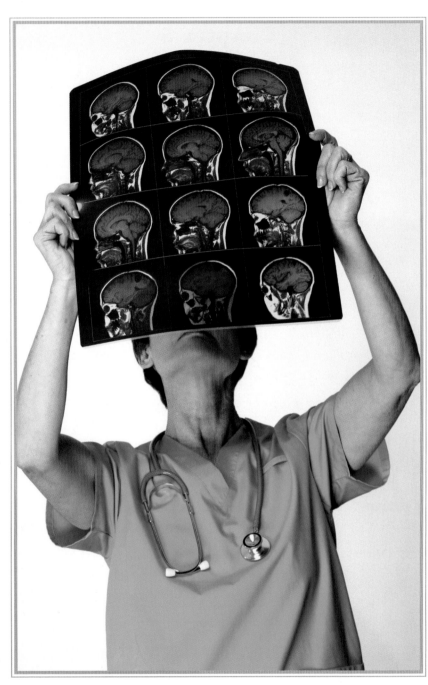

*A neuroscientist uses MRIs to create
visual images of the brain.*

Neuroscience

Neuroscience is the study of the brain; a neuroscientist is the scientist who studies the brain. A neuroscientist may specialize as a neurologist who diagnoses and treats brain diseases, as a neuroanatomist who studies the structure of the nervous system, as a neurochemist who studies the chemistry of the nervous system, or as a neuropharmacologist who studies the way drugs behave in and affect the nervous system, to name just a few specialty areas.

A neuroscientist must have skills that cross a diversity of disciplines. She must write research papers, give presentations about the results of her research, edit research papers that other scientists write, raise money to support her research by writing grant applications, and repair laboratory equipment. In short, she is a writer, public speaker, fund-raiser, and technician on any given day. If she works at a college or university, she is also a teacher.

Neuroscientists not only research and teach at colleges and universities, but also do independent research in government laboratories, work at pharmaceutical or biotechnology companies to develop new drugs, and work with and study patients in hospitals. While working in hospitals, a neuroscientist must be able to use many modern techniques to examine the brain. He will use magnetic resonance imaging (MRI), which creates a visual of the brain and helps him look for brain abnormalities or injuries; functional magnetic resonance imaging (fMRI), which allows him to view the brain in action; and positron-emission tomography (PET), which shows him activity inside the brain. He may use these tools to evaluate patients or to research psychiatric disorders, such as depression, and diseases of the brain, such as Parkinson's disease.

An organic chemist may work on developing new medicines.

Becoming a neuroscientist requires getting a bachelor of arts or bachelor of science degree in any scientific field from a four-year college or university; going to graduate school for a Ph.D. or finishing four years of medical or dental school; and finally, doing postdoctorate research on a particular scientific problem.

Neurology is an important department in all hospitals.

Want Ad:

Organic Chemist, Research and Synthesis

A high-profile pharmaceutical company with laboratories located in Amsterdam, the Netherlands, seeks full-time organic chemist to carry out original research in the field of research and synthesis. The organic chemist will produce on a large scale the drug compounds the discovery and development team design. The company will use these batches of compounds in preliminary clinical testing. The organic chemist will make sure the compounds are safe and pure before the company sends them to clinical trials. The applicant must have a Ph.D. in organic synthesis and at least one to three years' experience as a chemist at a pharmaceutical company or in the biotechnology industry. He must be a self-motivated scientist who has extensive experience with many different methods of synthesizing and isolating chemical compounds. Excellent communication skills are essential because he will work as part of a team.

A neurologist must complete even more years of education—up to seven years beyond a four-year college or university program. At a college or university, she will take pre-med courses in biology, chemistry, physics, and math to prepare for medical school. Once she has a bachelor of arts or bachelor of science degree, she will go through four years of medical school, a one-year internship, and a three-year residency program in which she treats patients in a hospital and studies

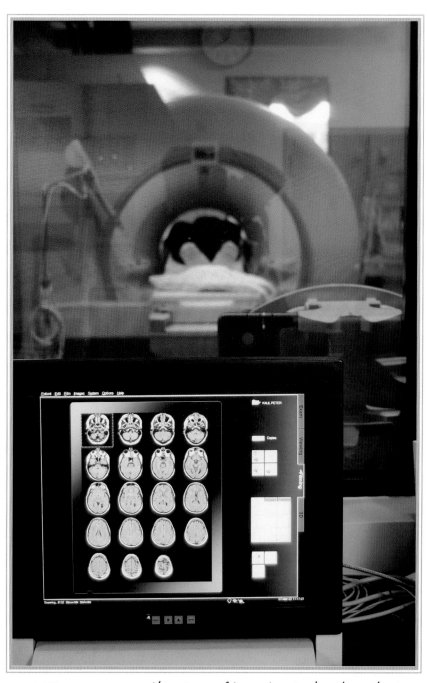

CAT scans are another type of imaging technology that allows a neurologist to look inside the human brain.

for a board certification exam. The board exam tests whether an aspiring neurologist has mastered all of the knowledge and skills she will need to practice professionally.

Synthetic Chemistry

A major type of chemistry involved in discovering and developing new drugs is called synthetic chemistry. Synthetic chemistry is the study of making new chemical compounds

A synthetic chemist may also be involved with working to develop new medications.

and is a branch of organic chemistry, the chemistry of compounds containing carbon atoms. Organic and synthetic chemistry are relatively recent developments in the field of chemistry. Chemists once extracted potentially useful compounds from plants or animals when looking for new medications; they could not produce new medicinal compounds in the laboratory. In the case of antidepressants, the discovery of

An organic chemist studies compounds containing carbon.

tricyclic drugs and MAOIs was lucky. When chemists could design and **synthesize** new compounds, however, this opened many more avenues through which scientists could research depression and its possible treatments. The SSRIs are products of organic synthesis.

An organic chemist is a scientist who studies the chemistry of compounds containing carbon. She may specialize in many different areas, but if she wants to work toward finding more effective treatments for depression, she will work in synthetic chemistry. In this field she will use her understanding of how chemical compounds behave and react under different conditions to design, synthesize, and develop possible drugs. She will use tools such as computer modeling to *simulate* chemical reactions and build new chemical compounds in three dimensions. Other techniques, such as nuclear magnetic resonance spectroscopy (NMR), which helps identify the structure and composition of newly synthesized compounds, and chromatography, which separates desired compounds from complex

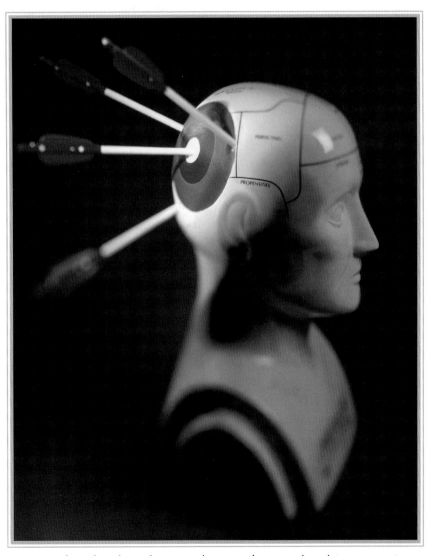

Many kinds of professionals may be involved in targeting treatments for neurological and psychiatric disorders.

A psychiatrist has both medical and psychological college training.

mixtures, are important to her work in the laboratory. When she produces a new drug, she will have to be sure of its structure, composition, and purity before it can proceed to preliminary trials.

To become an organic chemist who helps create new medications, she must first complete four years of college or university study. There, she will study biology, chemistry, engineering, physics, and mathematics, but she will focus on organic chemistry. She will study for up to five more years to get a master of science and a doctorate degree in a more specialized field such as organic synthesis.

Psychiatry

A psychiatrist is a medical doctor who diagnoses and treats patients with mental, behavioral, and emotional disorders. She is the physician who may prescribe and administer the medication other scientists develop to treat such disorders.

When a psychiatrist meets with her patient, she will do a routine physical examination as a medical doctor would do. She has the authority to order laboratory tests that she will interpret to find out whether her patient suffers from a psychiatric disorder, what kind of disorder her patient has, and the severity of the disorder. This information helps her form a treatment plan that may involve medication and/or psychotherapy. In psychotherapy a patient talks to the psychiatrist to try to resolve his problems.

A psychiatrist has at least eight more years of education to complete after receiving a bachelor's degree from a four-year college or university. She will spend four years in medical school, plus another four years doing a psychiatry residency, a hands-on program that trains her to treat patients and helps her prepare for her board exams.

After all those years of school, a psychiatrist must still pass a board exam to practice psychiatry. The American Board of Psychiatry and Neurology (ABPN) is one organization that creates and administers board exams. Organizations like the ABPN decide what knowledge and skills a psychiatrist must have before she can practice professionally. The ABPN works with the Residency Review Committees of the Accreditation Council for Graduate Medical Education (ACGME) to make sure residency programs prepare students for the board exam. Once a psychiatrist has passed her board exam, she must fol-

A psychiatrist may use talk therapy as well as medications when treating her patients.

low ABPN standards of treatment. Board exams make sure psychiatrists are well prepared to practice their profession, and therefore help protect the mental health of the patients the psychiatrists will go on to treat. Once she is certified, a psychiatrist may work in a private practice treating patients in an office setting, or she may work with patients in a public hospital. Psychiatrists may also do research or teach students. Psychiatrists may also receive further training that allows them to specialize in a particular field of psychiatry, such as child psychiatry, adolescent psychiatry, *geriatric* psychiatry, addiction psychiatry, or *forensic* psychiatry.

Psychiatrists are the professionals who ultimately receive and put to use the benefits of the research done by neuroscientists and chemists. The more neuroscientists uncover the mysteries of the brain, the more information biologists and chemists have to work with when they design new antidepressant medications. And, as a result, the more effective these medications will become in treating one of the most common mood disorders.

Further Reading

Barondes, S. H. *Better Than Prozac: Creating the Next Generation of Psychiatric Drugs.* New York: Oxford University Press, 2006.

Cefrey, Holly. *Antidepressants.* New York: Rosen Publishing Group, 2000.

Dudley, W. (ed.). *Antidepressants (History of Drugs).* Chicago, Ill.: Greenhaven Press, 2004.

Esherick, Joan. *Drug Therapy and Anxiety Disorders.* Broomall, Pa.: Mason Crest, 2004.

Esherick, Joan. *Drug Therapy and Mood Disorders.* Broomall, Pa.: Mason Crest, 2004.

Esherick, Joan. *The FDA and Psychiatric Drugs: How a Drug Is Approved.* Broomall, Pa.: Mason Crest, 2004.

Ford, Jean. *Surviving the Roller Coaster: A Teen's Guide to Coping with Moods.* Broomall, Pa.: Mason Crest, 2005.

Mitchell, E. Siobhan. *Antidepressants.* Philadelphia, Pa.: Chelsea House Publishers, 2004.

Parker, S. *The Brain and Nervous System.* London: Franklin Watts, 2002.

Shenk, J. W. *Lincoln's Melancholy: How Depression Challenged a President and Fueled His Greatness.* Boston, Mass.: Houghton Mifflin, 2005.

For More Information

American Chemical Society
www.acs.org

American Society for Neurochemistry
www.asneurochem.org

American Society of Neuroimaging
www.asnweb.org

Canadian Mental Health Association
www.cmha.ca

Center Watch: Clinical Trials Listing Service
www.centerwatch.com

Expedition Hope
www.ExpeditionHope.org

International Brain Research Organization
www.ibro.org

National Foundation for Depressive Illness, Inc.
www.depression.org

Neuroscience Canada
www.neurosciencecanada.ca

Neuroscience for Kids
faculty.washington.edu/chudler/neurok.html

U.S. Food and Drug Administration
www.fda.gov

Publisher's note:

The Web sites listed on this page were active at the time of publication. The publisher is not responsible for Web sites that have changed their addresses or discontinued operation since the date of publication. The publisher will review and update the Web-site list upon each reprint.

Glossary

apathy: Lack of enthusiasm or energy.

cognitive: Concerned with how knowledge is gained.

controlled: Carefully regulated.

convoluted: Very twisted, complex.

dynamism: Having the qualities of energy and action.

forensic: Having to do with the law and with crime.

geriatric: Having to do with the elderly.

hallucinations: The perceptions of someone or something being there when in fact they are not.

hemispheres: Halves of a sphere.

lobes: Rounded parts that project from the main body of something.

membranes: Thin layers of tissue.

mood disorders: A category of psychiatric disorders that pertains to state of mind.

optimistic: Having a positive attitude.

Parkinson's disease: A disorder of the brain that affects nerve cells, characterized by shaking and difficulty with movement and coordination.

peripheral: At the edge of something.

pessimistic: Having a negative attitude.

propagates: Spreads.

randomized: Arranged or selected in no specific pattern.

schizophrenia: A psychological disorder characterized by a loss of contact with reality.

simulate: Reproduce the features of something.

stimuli: Things that cause a response.

synthesize: Combine different elements into a new whole.

volts: Units of electric potential difference.

Bibliography

DePaulo, Jr., J. R. *Understanding Depression*. New York: John Wiley & Sons, 2002.

Emanuel, E. J., R. A. Crouch, J. D. Arras, and Moreno, J. D. Moreno. *Ethical and Regulatory Aspects of Clinical Research: Readings and Commentary*. Baltimore, Md.: The Johns Hopkins University Press, 2004.

Finger, S. *Minds Behind the Brain: A History of the Pioneers and Their Discoveries*. New York: Oxford University Press, 2000.

Icon Health Publications. *Antidepressants: A Medical Dictionary, Bibliography, and Annotated Research Guide to Internet References*. New York: Author, 2003.

Julien, R. M. *Primer of Drug Action*. New York: W. H. Freeman, 2002.

Martin, A. R., B. G. Wallace, and P. A. Fuchs. *From Neuron to Brain: A Cellular and Molecular Approach to the Function of the Nervous System, Fourth Edition*. Sunderland, Mass.: Sinauer Associates, 2001.

The National Institute of Mental Health. *Depression*. Bethesda, Md.: The National Institute of Mental Health, National Institutes of Health, U.S. Department of Health and Human Services, 2005.

Purves, D., G. J. Augustine, D. Fitzpatrick, L. C. Katz, A. S. LaMantia, J. O. McNamara, et al. (eds.). *Neuroscience, Second Edition.* Sunderland, Mass.: Sinauer Associates, 2001.

Schatzberg, A. F., and C. B. Nemeroff (eds.). *The American Psychiatric Publishing Textbook of Psychopharmacology.* Arlington, Va.: American Psychiatric Publishing, 2003.

Siegel, G. J., R. W. Albers, S. Brady, and D. L. Price (eds.). *Basic Neurochemistry: Molecular, Cellular and Medical Aspects.* New York: American Society for Neurochemistry, 2005.

Siegel, R. "Exploring Abraham Lincoln's 'Melancholy.'" *All Things Considered.* http://www.npr.com, October 26, 2005.

Wade, C., and C. Tavris. *Psychology.* Upper Saddle River, N.J.: Prentice Hall, 2000.

Index

Picture Credits

iStockphotos: pp. 15, 40, 52, 78, 98

    Eugeniy Meyke: p. 58

    Henrique Souza: p. 39

    Jan Bruder: p. 46

    Jan Kaliciak: p. 19

    Jose Gil: p. 95

    Kristen Johansen: p. 97

    Leah-Anne Thompson: p. 20

    Libby Chapman: p. 11

    Lisa F. Young: p. 23

    Luis Carlos Torres: p. 33

    Marcin Balcerzak: p. 100

    Marcin Laskowski: p. 36

    Mark Evans: p. 28

    Sharon Dominick: p. 66

Jupiter Images: pp. 8, 13, 16, 26, 35, 48, 57, 63, 72, 77, 81, 82, 84, 86, 89, 90, 92, 93

Malinda Miller: pp. 31, 43, 51, 55, 61

National Library of Medicine: p. 70

Biographies

Author

Maryalice Walker grew up in Falmouth, Maine. She is an alumna of Smith College in Northampton, Massachusetts. A 2004 Fulbright Fellow at the University of Cape Town (UCT) in South Africa, she currently studies bat ecomorphology in the UCT zoology master's of science program.

Consultant

Andrew M. Kleiman, M.D., received a Bachelor of Arts degree in philosophy from the University of Michigan, and earned his medical degree from Tulane University School of Medicine. Dr. Kleiman completed his internship, residency in psychiatry, and fellowship in forensic psychiatry at New York University and Bellevue Hospital. He is currently in private practice in Manhattan, specializing in psychopharmacology, psychotherapy, and forensic psychiatry. He also teaches clinical psychology at the New York University School of Medicine.